Meet
Remy.

Remy loves to eat. If you listed all of Remy's skills...

Chewing

Running

Eating

Eating would always be number one.

Remy has big ears.

Which are perfect for hearing when it's time to eat.

Sometimes, if Remy is extra good or does a fancy trick, he gets a special treat.

The **Cling**
of his treat tin
lets Remy know a treat is on the way.

Remy's food and treats make him very happy

But... Remy gets curious. He wonders from time to time if there are other things he could eat.

Popcorn on the Kitchen floor?
Remy thinks, "I could eat that!"

Out on a walk there's a
RUSTLE
RUSTLE

All the leaves on the ground,
Remy thinks, "I could eat that!"

A piece of paper fell out of the trash.

Remy thinks, "I could eat that!"

Running around with some friends at the park, Remy hears

Whoa. Remy's tummy is really full. More full than when he eats his food and treats.

Tummy aches are no fun. Remy thinks, "Maybe I shouldn't have eaten all that."

Good old dog food.

Made in the USA
Monee, IL
07 February 2020

21465721R00019